Praise for *The Light:*

"Janet's work resonates on many levels by giving the reader poems with tight weaves, rich colors, long echoes. She is one of the rare poets who is expressive and soul-searching, lyrical and eloquent, writing in the tradition of the Celtic bards. Her work is rich and inspiring, unique and amazing, and most assuredly... unforgettable."

~ Chris Dickerson, novelist, playwright and poet

Crossing the Severn River Bridge:
This is candid, transparent and yet so profoundly panoramic. There are a myriad of inferences that the reader may extrapolate from this simple, yet elegant write. You have made a connection simply yet profoundly without attempting to overpower the reader.

~David A. Neves

Sunday's Child:
A vibrant mix in which I see Monet crafted most eloquently not with paint but with deftly drawn words...

~Melanie Quigley Marquez

Perspective:
PERFECT title. There's a purity here, a simple clarity.
An innocence that's wonderfully appealing.   ~Chris Dickerson

Broken glass:
Powerful. This is one of those works where the words catch in mid-chest and grab hold.   ~Elaine Walmsley

Feather dreams:
This is a great poem, and that last stanza is as good as it gets.

~Chuck Steffen

Shades of Gray:
I love the textures and colors in this. It reads like an artfully enhanced black and white photo.   ~Leigh Spencer

Shades of Gray:
I really like the creativity of this; such a unique structure and conveyance.
~ Larry Kuechlin

Long time coming:
This reads like an eloquent power surge. I really like it, especially the last two lines. The feeling it evokes makes it hard to resist shouting "You GO, girl!"
~Leigh Spencer

Into the blue:
This poem is all the things that good poetry ought to be, a clear resonating voice leads the way. I LOVE the ending in particular, it's so human and revealing.
~Kimalisa Kaczinski

Into the blue:
This hits close to home, as you have met us at a place we all have been. It is never trite, over worn, haggard or too obvious, but yet is such a difficult part of the human experience, especially for a writer. Your courage and grace are inherent in this touching write. Thank you for another difficult but necessary slice of "daily bread".
~David Neves

For lack of a better word:
I like how your words paint the journey from lost to found from an expanse of space to the refuge of home.
~Maria Constanza Berardi

Universal Truth
I like the quiet nature of your voice here.
~Larry Kuechlin

Turning:
"Night kneels" before "sunset" and "sunrise". This makes this poem so complete, like a package that is a gift for the reader.
~Victor Claude Pirtle

The Light

Janet Scott McDaniel

FinnLady Press

Published by:
Janet Scott McDaniel & Chris Dickerson
FinnLady Press

ISBN-13: 978-1484036327
ISBN-10: 1484036328

Printed in the United States of America
ALL RIGHTS RESERVED

Photo Credits
© Jennifer L. Condron: pages 41,132,133 and back cover
© Janet Scott McDaniel: page 52
© Gregory Spiegel: page 60
© Cathia Mahaffey: page 70

The Light and other Collected Poems
Parallel Dreams
Tides

To the loved ones in my life who lift me up
and encourage me to fly, I say…

…. as you wish.

It is to them that I lovingly dedicate this book.

Introduction:

Let me start by saying that I never considered myself to be a poet.

When I wrote my first poem, *Footprints*, back in the 'dark ages' of the early 1970's, I thought it was a fluke; a one-time deal of: 'hey this isn't too bad.' To read it now, it strikes me as funny because I didn't have a first kiss or a date until I was 17 years old yet here I was, writing about a lost love at the age of 15.

Over the years I wrote a few more poems and never thought that writing poetry would be anything more than a lark, or a way to deal with my love and my heartaches. If I could capture the feelings I had and translate them into words on a page, then I could 'delete' them out of my heart, or so I thought, or preserve them so I could bring them to life in my mind later by reading them. As the years have passed I have captured many intense feelings, images, and beautiful memories.

There was a brief period in the mid-1980's when I wrote a few poems, but I hadn't put pen to paper in that way since that time ~ until November, 2010.

With the loss of my mother last November, I have begun writing poems again. Actually, it might be more accurate to say that the poems are *making* me write them!

The poems seem to be coming fast and furious, and while I am not as talented as famous poets I have read, or as prolific as current poets I have recently become acquainted with, for me to write a poem or two a week is amazing to me.

The 'lines' come to me at such odd times that I keep a notebook with me at all times, and also on my night table, often writing lines down in the dark as they come to me.

Let me tell you why I think this is....

Ten years ago Kelly, who is a friend of my son Greg, and is psychic medium, did a reading for me. It was the most amazing thing I have ever experienced! She described my family members and told me things that I had almost forgotten about; things that

Greg had no way of knowing, so I know that no prompting was involved. She told me that I am a portal to the other side, and can send and receive messages.

I have had many paranormal experiences in my life but they are increasing in frequency since my mother's passing. In the midst of all this, I am writing more poetry than I ever dreamed possible.

In going through my mother's papers in May 2011, my brother and I found a small notebook of poems that she had written in 1944-45, when she was 18 years old. We had no idea that she ever wrote poetry! In one poem there is the line, "I long to be a poet and inspire the world." That stopped me in my tracks.

I believe she is kicking up my creative energy now, sending me messages. Maybe she was never a recognized poet but I think she is determined to make sure that I am.

The way my work is evolving makes me believe that I am getting 'messages' from *somewhere*, for many of my recent poems are not feelings or images from my life.

This is certainly true in the poem *Legend* which is an image of a Dark Ages funeral for a royal figure. 'Legend' was written as a puzzle. I did not start out with a specific idea in mind for the poem. I got the beautiful 'lines' and pieced it together stanza by stanza just like working a puzzle. Only after I was finished did I go back to the beginning, read it through and realize what I had. Something akin to King Arthur's funeral, and immediately it said to me *Legend*.

The poem *The Petition*, a reference to a Celtic warrior princess, was written, line by line, while I attended a local auction. Every few minutes I would get another 'line' and scribble it into a little notebook I carry with me. A week later, it occurred to me that I should transcribe it before I lose the ability to make any sense out of what I had written in my book. When I finished typing it up into a document I read it through and realized the poem was complete and finished. I struggled with changing words, or 'polishing' the piece, but when I did it seemed to lose the power it had upon my first reading, so I left it alone. Sometimes you have to let poems be what they want to be.

8

I am of Scottish heritage and I have found that listening to Celtic music puts me in a 'zone' where the poems flow easier. The poem *Dark-Eyed Molly* came to be in this way. It literally wrote itself while I listened to Celtic music. I closed my eyes, Molly told me her story, and I wrote it down. For those interested, the The Celtic Mysteries CD by Roger Caverley, track number 5, Crowned in Ivy, is Molly's music. Look it up on the internet, and play that track while you read the poem and you will feel her.

In that same way, The Merlin Mystery CD by Alkaemy, track 9, Wand of Alchemy, is the music for my poem *Turning*. To me, the beauty of the poem is intensified by the haunting melody.

The journey to go public:

The catalyst to share my work publicly came from my son Gregory. He signed me up for an open mic night at a local coffee house, Espresso 'N Ice, here in my hometown. When he told me what he had done I laughed and said "Greg, I can't do that!" He replied, "You can , and you will, so bring your 'A' game. It's time you got your work out there. " So there you have it. I *had* to do it now… for my son.

To share my work outside of my family was an emotional risk for me. I am a 'sit in the corner and hide' kind of girl. I honestly didn't know if anyone would care about my writing besides myself, my friends, or my family. So, I gathered up what I thought were my three best pieces and read them at open mic night.

I read *The Light*, and *Free Fall*. The third poem I read that night is called *The Sign*. It is about a butterfly that lands to rest upon a warm rock, but finds the rock is actually the one who lifts it high and encourages it to fly. My son Greg did that for me. I would have never shared my work in a public forum if not for him. This entire journey is all because of the warm rocks in my life: those who lifted me up and encouraged me to fly.

To share my work and, therefore, my heart, is still a terrifying concept for me, but to know that my poems touch people's hearts ~ nothing makes me happier.

As for me, I seldom read, or fully understand most contemporary poetry because the elaborate wording, symbolism, and structure loses me. If I read it and don't "get it" right away, I don't enjoy it. So I tend to view my writing as 'a paper cup of plain vanilla ice cream' in a world of 'crystal dishes of rocky road with nuts and sprinkles'. You will add your own experiences to my work ~ your own nuts and sprinkles, so to speak ~ to make my poems uniquely yours.

I share with you here my images and heartfelt feelings, written in what I call my 'plain vanilla' style, yet still a rich tapestry of images. In this collection that spans 40 years of my writings I hope you will find a poem that will touch your heart.

With this book, and also as I say in my poem *Debut*: I give you my words, until you know my heart, no more secrets. I hope you enjoy the journey.

Janet

"*What is to give light, must endure burning.*"

~ Viktor Frankl

The Light

Resuming my creative kick after an almost thirty year hiatus-
to put the words together to form a poem from a "brilliant"
idea was a struggle….hence an idea.

I am NOT a poet

I am not a poet.
The words they do not flow.
They are pulled kicking and screaming
From the idea's afterglow.

****

I made my public debut as a poet on March 18, 2011, at
Espresso 'N Ice, a local coffee house here in my hometown.
The response was so overwhelming to me that I was still
awake at 3am, and I began writing my poem Debut.

I'll begin this book by finally saying, out loud:

"Yes….I AM a poet."

Debut

I wait
in a dimly lit room.
We each take our turn
amid the sea of unfamiliar faces;
with leaden feet
I walk to the gallows.

Sharing my soul
the noise fades to a whisper;
their eyes are hands
reaching for more.

I give them my words
until they know my heart.
No more secrets.

Transformation begins
for them,
and for me.

Our eyes flicker;
two hundred candles
in a dawn of understanding.

With a final breath
I am finished.
I wait.

It begins slowly
an avalanche
building to a thunderous roar.

I ride the wave of applause
all the way home.

I have been
Jack of all trades,
Master of none.

Tonight
I am master of one.
I am a poet.

My debut as a poet at Espresso 'N Ice. 3/18/2011

The Light

It's time to make the pilgrimage.
To re-charge. Renew.
Time to spend the hour's ride on the ferry.
Time to drive to the north side of the island.
It's time.
I am craving the solitude of the lighthouse
all alone on that tiny spit of land that carves its way
into the Atlantic Ocean where it meets Block Island Sound.
It's time.
I begin walking the mile long trek through the sand,
each step sucking the strength out of me
as waves lap against the rocky shore.
This is where I find my peace,
in the company of a solitary gull . . . alone.
The lighthouse is like a mirage
always seeming to be far away,
then suddenly the journey eases, and I am there.

And still I walk
past the lighthouse to the northern point of the island
where it slices like the blade of a knife
a half mile out into the water;
onto this blade I walk.
The Atlantic Ocean and Block Island Sound
crash together here, the water rising
in a hump in front of me where they meet.
Water stretching all around me,
as far as my eyes can see. . .
There with the waves lapping at my feet
I am a goddess standing on surface of the water.

I am the figurehead
on the prow of the boat which is my life;
face tilted skyward, arms outstretched
hair swirling around me
in the current coming off the ocean.

I am kissed passionately by the sun
as the wind runs its fingers teasingly through my hair.
I am inhaling deeply the power of the earth,
its life force beginning to course through my veins
more strongly now.
I feel the love for what has been,
what is, and what shall be.....
I feel the power.
I will chart my course.
I change tack. It's time.

I turn to begin the long walk back,
my eyes find the lighthouse, I see the light.
A friend once told me
'You are a light, you just don't know how bright you are.'
I smile and nod to myself...
I feel it now ~ the light in my eyes
guiding those I love as they chart their course;
showing the way to safe harbor in the storm.

The way is not long now, and I am strong.
I will be constant.
I will be bright.
I am the light.

North Light, Block Island, Rhode Island

When She Smiles

When she smiles

I am branded
her image burned into my mind
into my heart.

I come alive in her eyes, and
the world becomes
an afterthought.

When she smiles

My heart slams in my chest,
breath catches in my throat,
creating an empty silence
as the words fail to come.

My lips move trying to fill the void
yet her eyes say it all,
and silent I remain.

The years fall away,
and I feel it all anew

when she smiles.

Turning

Night kneels before a sunset sky,
streaks of burnished gold on her indigo skirt

her inclined head graced
by a moonlight crown

the nocturne of silver whispers
a luminous cloak upon her shoulders.

With rosy fingers
violet and indigo caress, intertwine

her pale starlight weaving in hushed tones
among ribbons of gold

an eternal dance in silken colors

greeting and parting in endless sighs.

Seconds breathe hours
as shadows wander in sapphire darkness

until turning

heartlong once again to greet wayward sun

night kneels before a sunrise sky,
streaks of burnished gold on her indigo skirt.

Perspective

Once again I wonder
how I will survive the storm
   of so much sorrow
   so much pain.
Raindrops hide the tears I've shed
   as I step into the rain.

A torrent of defeat tries to drown me
my breath I fight to gain
   as I begin to take a step
   or two
in the never-ending rain.

The storm rages overhead
   yet I realize I have learned
   not to wait for the storm to pass

I am changed.

I close my eyes
  and begin to dance
    in the rain.

Words

I stand in a healing rain
drinking deeply
of words once carelessly cast aside
by another's indifference.

I search them out as they fall from your lips;
splashing upon my face
warm and inviting, full of promise
no more sunsets
only sunrise.

I drink them in deeply to quench my thirst
that fire that burns inside,
as I slowly dry up
and crumble.

They flow into my depth
transforming this arid plain
into a tranquil valley, green, and lush,
fragrant with exotic flowers;
filled with the songs of the stream.

Glistening crystal drops that cling
to the delicate petals of the rose.

What was once a mirage in the distance,
a reflection of a memory
is a hypnotic rhythm that falls upon me now.

I smile
as the rain becomes one
with my tears.

The Sign

In a flurry of yellow and black
the tiger swallowtails flutter around the bush
laden with small white flowers
swaying gently in the breeze.

A heartbeat later
one alights upon my young
outstretched hand.

I am hypnotized by nature's magic
this small miracle which now sits upon my finger
its bright colors shimmering in the sun.

We stand there, the butterfly and I
    lost in the magic
    until I lift it up high
and blow gently under its flexing wings.

Suddenly.... it flies!...
fluttering in the gentle breeze
flying higher and higher.

I watch until it slips from view.

The sign comes to me a lifetime later
on a warm summer day
as I am kneeling in the flowerbed.

A tiger swallowtail dances across the yard
fluttering toward me
with sudden flashes of black and yellow
the first one I have seen since I was a young girl.

My breath catches in my throat
    as it comes ever closer.

I am in awe of its beauty once again
its colors brilliant in the sunlight.
It flies straight to me
this tiny messenger
and in that dream-like moment between breaths
      I see.
      I understand.

I wish it never to leave
but I know it belongs free on the gentle breeze
that carries it on its way.

Like the tiger swallowtail
I have been aimlessly fluttering
struggling against the wind in my life
    always searching
    until battered, and tired
I alight upon the warm rock to rest,
flexing my wings.

But to my surprise
I find that it's not a rock at all…
    it is the one who lifts me up
    to hold me high in the sunlight.

I feel the gentle breath under my wings
    willing me to fly
free to soar ever onward
to find my fulfillment.

I take the leap, and fly away
my brilliant colors shimmering
in the light that surrounds me,
for I know that the breeze will carry me
    ever higher.

One Perfect Moment

He gazes at me
the bewitching brown eyes make me tremble.
Enraptured by each other's presence
we stand
silent.

His strong hand
moves to gently touch my cheek;
warmth floods my body.

I press close
into the safety of his arms.

A gentle hand caresses my hair
and our lips meet in a whisper of a kiss.

To my dream I cling
as if to let go means death.

Why Must You Leave Me?

Why must you leave me?
How can I live
knowing you will be so far away
just beyond my grasp?

My dreams had become reality
and I knew the true meaning of life
and love.

Your memory will haunt me,
but memories will be all I have left;
cherished treasures in my heart.

Why must you leave me?
Distant cities summon~
you must heed their call.

But separation is not meant
for lover's hearts.

How can I live
knowing you will be so far away

just beyond my grasp?

Cold Gray Dawn

Standing in the cold gray dawn
Wondering if I was wrong
Trying to live my life without you.

Remembering the summer days
Laughing and loving until the morning haze
Finding after all this time...
    I still miss you.

I remember the look in your eyes
Things you said to me, and why
Not a day goes by
That I don't think about you.

Was it wrong of me to love you?
Was it wrong to need you so?
I found in your arms
The woman I'd lost
And a love I thought I'd never know.

Dawn breaks above a stone path in Edinburgh.

Free Fall

I cross the threshold
into the quiet of my room,
close my eyes,
step into nothingness;
a black void.

Free fall.

I lower myself onto my bed,
let it swallow me,
beginning a gentle spin that
rushes faster and faster
taking my breath away.
I am falling,
twisting and turning out of control.
What was up is down
and down is up
inside out, right side in.
What I thought I knew as right,
is all wrong, and the wrong is right.
I cannot change it
so I let go.

I drift in the blackness;
in the silence of a dead calm.
There is no place in time now.
The past rushes up to me
like a wave to the shore,
swirling, changing,
transforming to the present
and washing back out again
eroding my foundation,
fading again to black.

I am in free fall
until I make peace with my life
and open my eyes.

Long Time Coming

Destiny hurled us through the galaxy
and like the return of Halley's Comet
our worlds collided again today.

Newsflash!

My planet has shifted on its axis.

The black hole of you
the swirling maelstrom of unworthy
your gravity of subtle condemnation
did not pull me in.

I was the supernova that burned

RADIANT

leaving rays of disbelief
reflected in your eyes

and seeing that....

I burned brighter.

Crossing the Severn River Bridge

Twilight
driving alone in my car
Celtic music flowing from the radio

watching the blue sky
thinking of rain.

It always happens without warning

memories flood my heart
a tidal wave in a teacup

and still I drive.

The river stretches into the distance
and the sun sets beyond the horizon

where you are.

In the Twilight

Every now and again
the memory of that last goodbye
tho' decades past
pierces quick and deep
my heart beating to the rhythm of it

    "I'm leaving……"

The wrens returned this year
to build their nest in the willow tree.
He sings his love song to her
   and I smile.

A lifetime of choices made flash before me
and I will bear it
for I am given now
your bittersweet words upon the page

    "Maybe I should have stayed ……"

A postscript
making the reunion of our hearts
all the sweeter

A joining etched in stone
and a promise for a reunion of our hands

     someday.

I blow you a kiss to the man in the moon
                 and he smiles.

Shadowland

A sentinel
my fingers trace
lines on the windowsill

minutes turning into hours
as I keep vigil

certain that if I look long enough
hard enough
the never-ending sameness
will disappear
and I will see you walking
    ...coming to me.

The golden sun is sinking lower
dipping its toes into the horizon
in an ever-darkening sky

its cloak falling lightly upon my shoulders
as I turn
abandoning my watch.

Ever so gently,
an evening breeze pushes aside the lace
as it climbs in my window.

I close my eyes as its warm fingers
brush the bronze strands from my eyes

   trace the curve of my cheek
   slide slowly down my neck
   its breath upon my lips

and just for a moment
I let myself remember.

Tick-tocks echo from the hallway
marking the passage of the shadows.

Now I float through time
pale silk gown trailing behind me
through a silver pool of moonlight
spilling across the floor

green eyes glittering,
forever searching the darkness

yet all I can see
all I ever see

are your dark eyes watching
from the shadows of the past.

Lady Fair

On dusty road in deepening twilight
The gray palfrey prances
Toward castle towers piercing the sky
Upon which the moonlight dances.

Wrapped in velvet against the mist
Dewdrops clinging to her hair
Rides a heart with singular purpose
Within the lovely Lady Fair.

They ride through great iron portcullis
Past chiseled walls of stone
She alights, he does not whinny
The familiar journey, hers alone.

The massive carved wooden door
Creaks open on rusted hinges
Worn, faded tapestries adorn the walls
Her fingers lightly brush the fringes.

Embraced by ancient gray stone walls
While torchlight plays upon her hair
The staircase echoes in measured tones
The passage of Lady Fair.

From hidden pocket she takes the key
To the lock on the small arched door.
With trembling hand, she steps inside
Her silk gown rustles across the floor.

Upon the gilded table lies
The promise he gave to thee.
Lady Fair, as you gaze into the fire
Pray tell, what is it that you see?

Like spider silk, the slender thread
That binds him to her heart
On satin sheet she now lays her head
Crying softly in the dark.

Ten thousand suns have risen
Starry nights, silvery moons.
A whispering wind sighs… I love…
Truth conquers the web of gloom.

In fading light, she now journeys
On dusty road as if under a spell
Still a heart with singular purpose
Tho' now beating a death knell.

The castle walls, now crumbling
Her foot on well-worn stair
That leads to secret treasure
For the wizened Lady Fair.

Tower room, now dank and dusty
No warm and crackling fire.
She hobbles toward gilded table
Enraptured by heart's desire.

A shadow drifts across her face
She succumbs to the memory.
Withered hand holds a faded red rose
Lady Fair, I will be here for thee.

In the cloak of deepening twilight,
Her head bowed as if in prayer
A single tear falls
From the eye of Lady Fair.

Contemplation

If you are in need
I will give all that I have.

If you need help
I will help you in every way that I can.

If you need love
I will love you with all of my being.

I am not to be won
I am freely given.

I am sweet
waiting in a sour world.

I see
waiting to be seen.

I am understanding
waiting to be understood.

I am a treasure
waiting to be treasured.

I am patient
waiting
for you.

Daydream

I faltered

just for a moment,

tripped over today
and fell headlong into daydream;

skinning my knees
on all the what-ifs left behind.

I roll over
and with a sigh of resignation
I find myself floating
upon the Maybe Sea,

   surrendering

to the gentle rocking of:

   would-have-beens
   could-have-beens
   might-have-beens

while in the quiet of never-was

I watch the if-onlys
float lazily across the sky

   and drift away.

Bubbles

Memories
Floating like iridescent soap bubbles
colors swirling.

Some large, some small
sometimes held together
in an unbreakable bond

drifting away

until the gentle breeze of time
pushes them back toward me
and I see them anew.
   Whole.
   Complete.
   Perfect.
Their colors swirling
shifting and changing.

It's then I remember
I see the world with child-like eyes.

Sunrise
sunset
and moments in-between

life and love
each and every one
new and wondrous in my eyes.

Each one a treasure
encased in a bubble.

They float back to me now.

I watch them in amazement
with my wide child-like eyes

    until they burst

    and are gone

scattering their wondrous colors
    in my mind

until they appear again

    floating

in the gentle breeze of time.

I Walk Alone

I walk alone
in school without friends
into the black void of loss
and loneliness
   without my father
   without a boyfriend.

I walk alone
in the shadow of a marriage
with my children
without a best friend.

I walk alone.

Days wash up on my shore
slip back out again
an endless sameness
turning into weeks
          months
          years.

I walk alone
   without a mother,
   without a spark to warm an aching heart;
   without the one.

I walk alone.

Sucked into the past
through a worm hole in time
spit out again into the present
holding tightly to the ember
feeling its warmth grow
lighting the darkness within.

I walk alone, no longer.

Footprints

Footprints, you remind me
of a love lost long ago
when I walked with my love,
across the beach so slow.

This little bit of love
that was left behind,
had somehow slipped
out of my mind.

You trail across the beach
where we once walked
and linger at the spot,
where we both talked.

Something seems very strange
this time.

This time
the footprints are only mine.

The Stone

You were handsome,
  smart,
  funny,
  comfortable in yourself

a brilliant wordsmith,
a bright light.

Oh, how I longed
for that light to shine
on me.

I was the shy one,
  quiet,
  insecure,
  lonely.

A stone
among the glittering diamonds
that surrounded you.

Then came the brief moment
when I felt the light,
    the heat
    upon my face.

In your eyes
I was a colorful Hope,
a radiant Cullinan
sparkling colors of the rainbow.

Too soon the moment is lost
and I am again in darkness;
warm from the heat
  yet still a stone.

Time has floated us apart

Your light to the west
    a rare jewel
cut, polished and radiant

     sparkling

among the myriad of diamonds on the shore.

From this wordsmith I have read
and so learned a universal truth.

No pirate's cross was above me.

Never was I to inspire words
    of longing or desire
    words of aching need
    or passionate love

    or of love lost.

The inspiration
came from the diamonds
that surrounded you

I am
    …but a stone.

The stone still lies to the east
    worn
    yet still familiar;
    still a comforting presence.

With the rising sun
I feel the light,
    the heat.

Here
I inspire no passionate words
        only a low moan

no eloquent aching need
        only misty eyes.

My paso doble
        is a trembling embrace.

Here
I sparkle colors of the rainbow.

Here
I am transformed into a diamond

        among stones.

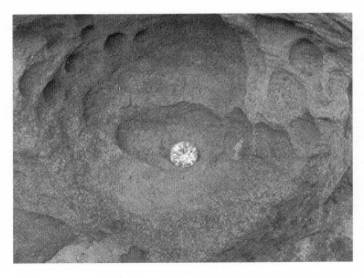

Magic Eyes

Magic Eyes
Searching my face
Searching my soul
Filled with emotion
Losing control

Holding me tightly
Trembling embrace
Setting me free
Love on his face

There are no secrets
Nowhere to hide
I came to life in those
Magic eyes

Dark-Eyed Molly

Spring's morning sun shrugs off
its cloak of night
Stretching rosy fingers into a violet sky
Gently pushing aside the morning mist
That clings tenderly to golden moors.

Long rays of pale yellow light
Reach out like a yearning lover
To touch the solitary figure crowned in ivy
Walking upon a narrow gray stone path
Winding its way through the highlands.

Dark-eyed Molly walks.

A gentle breeze brushes away her tears
As downcast eyes watch the passage
Of cold stones beneath her feet.
Not seeing a world waking around her
She listens only to the rhythm of her heart;
Her steps echo its beating.

She walks, past thistles covered with dew
Murmuring words of love;
Willing them to be borne upon the wind
Like arrows shooting through the sky
To pierce the heart of he who stole hers.

Dark-eyed Molly walks.

By blackthorn tree on far away hill, she lingers
Face tilted toward summer sun's embrace
As warm as her imagined lover's touch.
Eyes closed, she whispers
her impassioned plea...
                    Come back to me.

White clouds drift across the azure sky
Heather bow, and sway, in the gentle breeze
Redwings, and bramblings sing.
There, lost to the world's majesty

Dark-eyed Molly walks.

The orange sun sinks into a deepening sky
Shadows lengthen upon the autumn hill.
Muffled voices float up to greet her
As amber lights wink on in the valley below
Drawing her ever nearer.

Past the town's massive stone gate
Lanterns are lit, she hears the laughter
Hidden in darkness she silently watches
Bowing her head, her gaze drifts away.

Dark-eyed Molly walks.

Pale ribbons of moonlight illuminate the way
Dark emerald forest whispers its greeting
Sharing its mysteries of secret trysts
Shadows shifting, changing before her eyes.

Silver rays of moonlight now embrace her
Stroking her hair, playing upon her lips.
She hugs her cloak tightly around her
Longing for a warmth she will never feel.
Under the watchful gaze of the
Winter Scottish moon

Dark-eyed Molly walks.

This poem was unexpected. Molly came to me and began to tell her story. The images came while listening to Roger Caverley's Celtic Mysteries CD. One particular track brought her into vivid focus for me. With "her" music playing, I closed my eyes, and Molly took me for a walk and told me her story.

Only after I finished this poem did I find this information:
Brigid - called 'Bride' in Scotland - the Pagan Celtic Goddess of healing, home and hearth, fire, inspiration and creativity.
The image of Brigid shows her wearing a crown of ivy.
The title of the track that I felt was "Molly's music" is called Crowned in Ivy.

I had no inkling of any of these things when I wrote the poem.
I only know that the music spoke to me of Molly, and the images came. Did Brigid help me to "see" Molly's story through her eyes? You tell *me*....

Sunday's Child

The painting hangs in a corner
overlooked
until you move closer.

The frame is soft gold
simple yet elegant
just enough to highlight a canvas
where on a tranquil blue background
vibrant colors dance
with wild abandon.

Two intense orbs of emerald green
cast a spell, drawing you near.

Bold swirls of sun-kissed yellow
playfully intertwine with tender touches
among the forgiveness of violets
and forget-me-nots.

An eclectic mix
lovingly woven together
it beats with a life of its own
calling to your heart

forever changing as you move closer.

From one minute to the next
always a surprise.

Legend

In a shroud of foggy mist
with tears dripping from the trees
a heart beats hard and fast
yet still the falcon falls
its scales tipped to darkness.

Torchlight flickers as it listens
to whispers in the wind, held
in the caress of raven's wings
suspended between one realm and the next
as the waves roll to shore
in an endless procession.

Soon flaming shadows will cross the sky
arcing toward the distant funeral pyre
as it drifts upon dark water; moving
ever closer to the translucent veil.

In that time between times...
sorrow and life go hand-in-hand.

Now, among ribbons of moonlight
with her legion she stands silent upon the shore
watching...

Luminous green eyes gifted with second sight
tell the tale, for they knew the worth in the blood.

In vindication
banners rise in tribute under a star-filled sky
and their voices echo the truth

Flickering candlelight hides the flaws
that sunlight shows so raw.

The Petition

I petition my warrior protector
Train this eager apprentice
To be a warrior princess

Give me the shield
To deflect words that wound

A sword with which to parry
Deeds that threaten to destroy

Armor to protect from
Venomous arrows that inflict pain
And death

Transform a shy smile
Into a fierce countenance
Projecting strength
Inspiring fear

To rise in your image of defiance
Invincibility

Train me
To defend against those who seek
to use me for their own devices

Make me
A warrior princess equal in combat
With her warrior

Make me
In your image
For then you can never hurt me.

Rules

I scurry about
a hungry little mouse
looking for crumbs
   finding only vibrant petals
   fragrant blossoms
   the bouquets tossed at her feet.

Alone and weary
needing warmth
I scurry on
     past a cat
       sleeping on her favorite chair
              by the fire.

And still I search,
still waiting to find

   crumbs

among the rules.

57

The Empty House

The empty house beckons to me
eerie and foreboding
in the moonlight.

The winds icy fingers
seem to urge me on
and I enter.

The air of decades past
weighs heavily upon my shoulders.

Apparitions dance
among the forgotten memories.

A hollow sadness
clutches at my heart.

Silvery webs
apparitions wisping across the walls
the dust of my ancestors
bids me stay
     …belong.

Miss Scarlett

I had started to write a poem about my car, a muscle car, and while on the way to work *Sweet Freedom* came on my cd. *Sweet Freedom,* the incredible feel-good song sung by Michael McDonald. Whenever I hear that song it courses through my veins like a drug high, bringing me to life.

I thought ... dang! ... this is such a *GREAT* song, and I played it over and over all the way to work. I left work and was meeting my son Greg for lunch. I played *Sweet Freedom* all the way to Olive Garden, and when I pulled in the parking lot, what do I see? My car!!! Greg had driven it to work.

That's when I realized that the poem can only exist with the car AND the song. That's how they exist in my mind. The power for me is in the two together.

Rewind to May 1990. I bought a red 1987 Firebird, 5 speed, and drove the hills of Connecticut for hours with that song playing on the car stereo, as therapy during my divorce. It healed me and set me free. I traded that car in for a sedan the next year, doing the "right thing". Big mistake. Broke my heart.

Fast forward to May 2000. I can't stand it any longer. I need to run the gears. Car dealers tell me, "Sorry, I can't help you, stick shifts are hard to find." So, internet here I come. Only now, I decide to go for the brass ring. I want a Firehawk, a limited edition Firebird where they bump up the horsepower, tweak the body a bit and give her special graphics. And I want red. And a stick.

So, I do a search on eBay and the only Hawk listed is exactly what I want. 1994. Red. Six speed. Graphite leather interior. I call the seller, buy her, purchase a one way plane ticket to Louisiana and drive her the 1200 miles home.

Miss Scarlett is my therapy. It is no accident that she is named for Scarlett O'Hara. She is beautiful, sexy, devious, and so deceptively powerful. She is a siren who calls to me. You can't feel bad when listening to that throaty rumble and running the gears. Especially when you put Michael on the car stereo and turn up the volume.

Let me introduce you to:

Miss Scarlett

1994 Pontiac Firehawk #471

Miss Scarlett

I open the door to greet her
Sleek, low, menacing;
Deliciously sexy.
Blood red in the morning light;
Dark leather beckoning
Miss Scarlett says,
Come.... *take* me.

I slide inside her
With a deep thud she closes around me;
We fit together like Lego blocks.
Gently I slide the key into her,
Turning;
She suddenly roars to life
Three hundred horses screaming;
Settling back into a throaty rumble
Begging me to feel their power
To set them free
So I do.
Sweet Freedom
Turn it up.
Loud.

The first bars bring me to life
Coursing through my veins
Like a drug high.
Michael's baritone wooing me...

No more running down the wrong road
dancing to a different drum
Can't you see what's going on
deep inside your heart?

Always searching for the real thing
living like it's far away
Just leave all the madness in yesterday

You're holding the key
when you believe it

I push in the clutch
Deftly feeling for first
Gently sliding into gear
Ah…there it is…

Ease off the clutch
Give her some gas
She comes to life in my hands
Responding to my touch
Shuddering
As I punch into second
Third.

Shine sweet freedom
Shine your light on me
You are the magic
you're right where I want to be
Oh sweet freedom carry me along
We'll keep the spirit alive on and on

We move as one.
I guide her through the curves
The afternoon sun warm on our bodies
As we dance together
The countryside a blur
Hair flying in the wind
Smoothly shifting
As I feel my way into fourth.

We'll be dancing in the moonlight
smiling with the rising sun
Living like we've never done
going all the way

She is throbbing under me.
I ride the hills and valleys
Like waves at sea
Lost in her.
Golden sun dips low into a violet sky
I am pushing her hard
Slamming her into fifth.

Reaching out to meet the changes
touching every shining star
The light of tomorrow is right where we are
There's no turning back
from what I'm feeling

Her throaty roar mounts
Like a wild animal.
She screams into sixth;
Straight up to the red line,
Rocketing down the road
Until we almost fly.

'Cause there'll be starlight all night
when we're close together
Share those feelings dancing in your eyes
Tonight they're guiding us
shining till the morning light

Oh, sweet freedom…..

Sweet Freedom lyrics © Rodney Temperton
Sweet Freedom sung by Michael McDonald.

If Wishes Were Horses

If wishes were horses, beggars would ride
And oh how I *wished* to be
Fair maiden who charms the
Handsome prince
But alas, t'was was not to be.

The prince and I were of like minds
No lack of conversation
Still, as we lounged by crackling fire
I was conscious of my station.

Too soon he traveled far and wide
To strange and exotic lands
In search of her who knew his heart
And to whom he'd give his hand.

Maidens dark, or fair, with flashing eyes
From every town they came
The prince he charmed them all, you see
Tho' he never asked their name.

He failed to return victorious
In matters of the heart
His mind kept drifting back to the one
Waiting at the journey's start.

The crowds they cheer, and roses throw
You ask, how this could be?
The Prince now rides upon his white horse
And beside him there rides… me.

Free Flight

In the stillness of daybreak,
washed by early morning light
we unfurl the envelope,
and position a giant fan
that begins to breathe life.

A sleeping beast rudely awakened,
the envelope begins to snap and undulate,
billowing in ocean-like waves,
lifting slowly from the ground.

With a loud hiss the burner ignites,
sending a flaming dagger
deep into its open mouth.
It tosses its head and begins to rise,
dwarfing us
as we stand watching

The envelope strains
against the cables of the gondola
as we climb inside.

With a burst of fire we rise into the air,
our shadows transforming
on the terrain below.

The silence is deafening.

We are the wind.

In the Eye of the Beholder

The rain falls in torrents,
wind lashing the car as you drive on,
the road empty;
passing a steady stream of cars.

Evacuation.

From her stunned lips you hear
the same words over and over
'You're driving me into a hurricane'.

Your room awaits-
the one you always have in that
quaint little B&B at the beach.

All through the night the storm rages on
giving way to a brilliant sky
a desolate beach, almost a perfect memory
only you're without her now.

We're different, you and I
different from what has come before
different from what could ever be.

We will challenge the storm with raised fists
traveling against the tide to where our room awaits
    eyes twinkling
while the storm rages through the night
making our perfect memory
under a brilliant sky, on a desolate beach
    together.

My darling…
    anytime
    anywhere
    drive me into the hurricane.

Bella, the little one left behind.

As I Leave

Come here my darling little one
Come cuddle close by me
I need for you understand
I need for you see

That I love you deep and true
My heart has found a treasure
Beyond what I thought possible
Beyond what I can measure

In your eyes such innocence
Such sweet and trusting grace
A love unconditional and pure
A love that radiates

How do I tell you, little one
Life's road takes me away
That leaving you is not easy
That I am counting the days

I know you do not understand
A single word I say
I cannot change what will come
I cannot take heartbreak away

So cuddle close my darling one
I know your heart will pine
Someday, my memory will fade
Someday, we'll *both* be fine

Ghosts in a Machine

A rising sun shoots arrows of light across
the keyboard as fingers tap away,
a second cup of coffee at the ready, then
when least suspected, she appears with
a mischievous smile that plays upon her lips;
eyes twinkling with merriment, as she sits atop the piano,
long legs draped over the keyboard.

"Enough already! There's work to be done." but
sometimes she twirls with arms outstretched,
holding veils that swirl around her naked body,
playing peek-a-boo with the curves beneath.

"Now cut that out!", but she's not listening,
for the game is in the distraction.
Long dark hair frames sultry eyes that
speak of the fire within; she's voluptuous in
a little black dress and stilettos, lying
across the top of a red leather sofa.

Double take. "Gorgeous gypsy girl…"
Smiling, she transforms again, as
under a mop of dark hair, her pale face looks
up with mesmerizing big blue eyes, the
lanky frame suggestively curled on the floor.

Sharp intake of breath as the words slow
to a drip, and seen through misty eyes, she is
much older now, yet she still smiles that
big smile from years ago, a fur coat
draped around her shoulders, floating

with the sirens on the screen,
frozen in time; forever to remain
    ghosts in a machine.

Goodbye

Our marriage ended today.
I still can't believe you walked away.
Didn't the vows we took when love was new
Carry the promise of a lifetime for you?

I believed that love could conquer all
And be there to catch you if you fall.
You've shown me that in spite of heart and soul
A man's love can turn stone cold.

Snow Blind

She equated it with being snow blind.

What began as a beautiful thing
evolved into something corrosive
insidious in how it spread
        became uglier
  more vile in its sweetness.

She made excuses for his behavior
thinking
next time I will come first
next time he will lift me up
next time I won't be dismissable
maybe
next time.

And still she wondered
when will I be more important
than money
or things?

As her slender shoulders bore
an ever-increasing burden
    the poison spread
    her spirit succumbed
a slow death of the psyche.

Turning her back to the snow
she closed her eyes…
his words still sweet
yet their underlying message
    unchanged.

The toxic nature so very clear
as her eyes opened.

Degrees

I know it for a fact.
I know it to be true.
You'll never love me
as much as I love you.

You often say the words,
you believe you do your part;
but the most that you could ever do,
for me, it would only be a start.

I try hard every single day
to show my love for you each minute,
and even though I know you mean to,
I wait for you to begin it.

It's not enough to speak the words
That, any fool can manage.
It's words without actions
that do irreparable damage.

I wait for you partner up
for doesn't that define marriage?
But day by day I carry the burden,
my actions you disparage.

So while I wait, heart in hand,
to be swept into your arms of love,
you hold back, like I'm fragile,
like you have to wear kid gloves.

So, I know it for a fact.
Sadly, I know it to be true.
You'll never love me
as much as I ... loved you.

The Accolade

Magic begins on a warm May day
when the sun gently kisses her as she runs
with leaps and twirls of joy, among
the crazy quilt of colors spread upon the ground.

"Daddy, look!" she calls out
as she spies another treasure, and

as she marvels at the beauty around her
I am drawn into her world. She reminds me
of the simple joys that surround us;
the ones my eyes sometimes no longer see.

"Daddy, come quick!" and I run to see
what mystery I will explain, because

in her adoring eyes I am the oracle. I am her warrior
against the creatures of the dark; her guide
through the symphony of the shaded forest.

I am he who would be king,
  with a dandelion crown.

"Daddy, I have presents for you!"
As she comes running, I realize once again
I love her down to the ground, up to the stars
and beyond the horizon.

I kneel before her.

My eyes mist as I receive the accolade of my princess
for into my cupped hands she gently places
rocks and buttercups.

Oh, My Love

Oh, how peaceful is the night
as thought we are cloaked
in a soft, dark blanket
the sounds of the world muffled
your body warm and inviting
against mine.

Wrapped in each other's arms
we lie so very still.
with each breath, I feel you move
ever so slightly.

You sigh a contented sigh
I watch the moon
run silvery fingers through your hair
your handsome face serene.

Oh my love
envelope me in your virility!

Let us share the secrets of our souls
until our cloak of night is lifted
by the rosy fingers of dawn.

The Last Real Hero

Fighting not with guns or knives
still, he fought
slaying monsters
under the bed.

Fighting not with fists
he battled her injustices
suffered on the schoolyard
great and small.

Fighting not with angry words
he righted the wrongs
that caused her tears
or tried to.

Fighting not only with medicine
but with every cell of his being
he fought to stay with her.

Devotion in his eyes
never wavering
as it should be.

Her father
the last real hero.

In Memory of Dad

Familiar faces, tear-filled eyes
A million empty words
An ache deep inside.

Hundreds of flowers
Fill the room.
The fragrance of love
And deepest gloom.

Sleepless nights
A sightless stare
An empty life,
A bad nightmare.

Alone in a crowd
Hearts filled with despair.
A part of me died,
My Dad is not there.

Written in 1972, in loving memory of my father:
James Kenneth Scott   June 30, 1926 - May 17, 1972

Into the Blue

When I feel the warm sun upon my face each year on a day in May just after my birthday, the one thing I remember so vividly is the blue plastic bag lying on the car seat between us. I talked about my day at high school on the ride home, but I only remember two of her words: heart attack. We visited Dad that night in the CCU, and I saw death on his face, in spite of the reassurances. Within those fleeting 30 minutes, Dad said he could not have had a better daughter. Mom wrote down the instructions that he dictated to her. He was a college professor and was worried about his classes. That breaks my heart now. None of us said, "I love you". I told him I would see him in the morning. It was an aneurysm, and there was no morning. At the viewing, I remember his students weeping inconsolably as I stood there numb. Mom never re-married. I told Mom I loved her. She died this year. Her last words to me as she touched my face were, "You're so pretty". My brother and I cleaned out her house, our childhood home. Throughout my life I have always been called Janet. I found a note Dad had written to me. He called me Jan.

From the Far Side

From the far side she comes to me
Her soul wraps around my heart
I am transported to a place
of immeasurable grief
I feel the loss, the pain, the sorrow.

There is no world in this moment in time
A lifetime of love closes around me
holding me close

Our souls touch, for I feel her with me
guiding, loving, protecting
A bond beyond life
a final farewell

In a heartbeat she leaves me
forever touched
by the power of her love

In loving memory of my great-aunt: Ann Elizabeth Selby
May 9, 1908- December 14, 1989

Vision

Timeless
is our journey, walked
within a circle of minutes.

Eternal
is our love, measured
by the flutter of heartbeats.

Never-ending
the thread of emotions
that weave our soul's tapestry.

Passionate
our desire to live, to give love
and to receive it.

Forever
the whispering in our ear,
the longing which is eternally ours

Hope
that our eyes will recognize
the angels that walk among us.

Illusion

Oh, the anticipation!

Memories of smiles
twinkling eyes
and warm gentle arms
are tossed in the whirlwind
of my thoughts

Oh, the anticipation!

Coming face to face again
with the dream that stirs my soul

The unattainable dream
   so real
   so sensual
   so comforting
yet so fragile it must be sheltered
from the thought of reality

Oh, the longing!

for a few precious moments
when I can hold
and caress my dream
when I become so lovely
   so alive
   so sensuous
that my heart cannot contain it

Oh my dream!

My life!

My love!

I cannot surrender you to reality

Damning myself to a world
     where I am cared for
     but not loved

Living in a void
   with your face before me
   and the memory of your lips
   hot upon my own

You are not my dream
   you are my reality
   and my life is my nightmare
   from which you have rescued me

   if only for a moment

   and given me love

For Jennifer

Welcome ~ our firstborn child !
Now that the months
of waiting have passed, and the pain ended
you are here.

Wrapped now in a blanket,
and looking small and frail
in your Daddy's arms
as you intently study his face.

Just minutes into the world
yet your tiny hand holds
tightly to my finger.

How strange we are to you.

Thrust out of darkness
into light and sound
finding you must breathe and eat
on your own.
Struggling against the
confinements of clothes,
how cruel the world must seem.

You cry
venting your frustration and exhaustion.
I cradle you gently in my arms.

Sleep comes quickly
and I stroke your soft dark hair
admiring the long dark lashes.

God could not have created
a more angelic face
free from the troubles of life.

I wish you contentment always
my precious baby girl.

The Search

I've got to find "me",
please try to understand.

My life is in turmoil,
so many things are changing
I've got to find my destiny.

I want to love you,
but how can I know love
when I no longer know myself?

Be patient with me
I also hurt deep inside
so much pain and anguish
must be forced aside.

When I know my true feelings
I will come willingly …joyfully.

No reservations.
No hesitations.

With a heart full of love and desire
such as you have never known.

Be patient with me.

I must be secure within my
own feelings
before I can be secure
within yours.

Blink

on tiptoe
autumn plays
golden
peek-a-boo

green leaves
nod
flush crimson

cling
to branches
waving
in autumn's breath

release
their hold
falling
in quiet hush

whisper
to winter winds
peeking
in a northern sky.

No Turning Back

Dark clouds are passing overhead
stormy thoughts drifting
through my mind
the reflections of a troubled heart.

Like the clouds
there is no turning back
no retreat to better days
when rosy fingers reached high into the sky
bringing life and warmth
as did my lover's arms.

The chill wind drives the clouds
violently across the sky.

I turn away
whipped by the wind
begging for the hurt to be driven
out of my heart
for there is no turning back.

No re-living of sun-filled days
love-filled eyes
candlelight dancing upon the face
which was my life
my love.

Rain,
wash these tears from my face
refresh my soul.

I must begin anew,
looking only toward the future,
for there is no turning back.

Autumn

Autumn has come.
The leaves flaming with color
mirror my heart burning with desire.
A cool wind rustles the leaves
and the chill of loneliness pierces my heart.
Tears sting my eyes
as the wind carries the leaves away.
They are so like my love;
the hidden and sleeping desires
bursting into bloom, incredibly vibrant
radiating the joy of living.
So I have lived this summer…
love fanning my passions into fiery glory.
Autumn has come.
The dying leaves are tossed by the wind
but their life lies dormant;
their renewal will come again.
So must my love lie dormant;
my passions will lie hidden,
never ceasing
until you, my spring
                              …return.

All I Am Not

A lifetime
of patiently waiting,
yet so tired of wanting

needing

asking

pleading

as you quietly ignore.

Ragged teeth tear at my soul

My glass heart shatters
as I receive your answer

an empty silence.

Still
here I lie

silently writing you
my dreams in the dark.

I am the heart easily broken
who has cried a river of tears.

I am drowning
in all I am not.

New Year's Eve

The clock counts down toward midnight
persistent in its insistence
that I be made aware
of each moment as it passes.

of each moment that came before
of each moment still to come
of each moment that was empty
of each moment that was full
of each moment of despair
of each moment of hope
of each moment of preparation
of each moment of reflection
of each moment of solitude
of each moment spent lonely
of each moment spent alone
of each moment of companionship
of each moment of laughter
of each moment of kindness
of each moment of compassion
of each moment spent in gratitude
of each moment filled with love.

In Quiet Places

Lined up, soldiers in a row
Bindings worn, standing ready

Waiting

Aged, ageless
The past, the future
Held tall with pride

Bookends

Stoically shouldering
The burden.

From One Jan to Another

A golden sun rises, beginning another day
and I realize that I am privileged
    to be alive
    to be healthy
    to be.

I am conscious of how easily I can take a breath
how glorious to feel the oxygen
coursing through my body,
my heart pumping strong
and never-ending
  or so it seems.

Minutes pass, turning into hours
  and once again
I am acutely aware that miles away,
Jan fights for her life.

She fights nobly,
with unparalleled grace of spirit
the most difficult fight
to die with dignity
showering those she loves so very dearly
with love in each of her words,
  in each touch.

But each journey must come to an end.
We get the news she has crossed the threshold
and taken her place in time.

Suddenly life seems paler as the bright spark
 that lit our small corner of the world goes dark.

Life has a way of dropping you to your knees;
in pain at her loss
yet grateful for having known her.

The memories come unbidden.
I can see her warm smile even now
   radiant
   genuine
as we sit in the front row at the auction,
her eyes twinkling with amusement as we tease her;
she is grinning,
waving her hand in a dismissive fashion
saying,
         "Oh, *stop*!'

never meaning a word of it
the laughter overtaking us all.

I remember her unbridled joy
as she bought trays full of costume jewelry
spending the next hour
      or more
intently looking,
      and marveling at each ordinary piece.

   To me, they were worthless;
   to her, each one was a treasure.

   Jan *created* the magic.

When I replied to her question,
 "What's going on in your life?"
she listened
      ... *really* listened.

How rare to be truly heard by another person.

         Jan heard you.

When I shared the dire condition of a friend with her,
she used her wealth of knowledge as a nurse
   to guide me in order to help my friend

98

to make a difference
        and she did.

To her, no one was a stranger,
        only a long lost friend.

            Jan was selfless.
It manifested in her spontaneous giving.

I sometimes carry a purple leather purse.
    It became mine after I shared with Jan
the story about my husband bidding on the wrong purse.
I thought it was funny that he could mistake black
            for purple.

She had bought the purse I wanted,
but I didn't know that
until she brought it the next week
and gave it to me.

That gesture might have baffled some people,
but not me
because I knew her.
She wanted those around her to be happy.

Random acts of kindness one could say
only with Jan,
            not so random.

They were given every day
                    ...everywhere.

Now the sun has set
and night descends upon us.

I am humbled by the gift of life.
No...
        by much more than that

I am humbled by the gift of *Jan's* life.

Because I knew her, I am changed.
The memories will linger.

I will find laughter again, even though the tears.

I will carry within me the light of her spirit

  her strength of character
  her pure goodness.

She taught me to face life with kindness and grace
and always
 always
   with laughter.

I will do you proud, my friend
for I have your example to follow
as I continue on in my journey through life,
and I can hear you say, "You go, girl!"

You echo back to me now.

A smile tugs at my lips as my son teases me
until I am grinning
and I find myself dismissing him
with a wave of my hand
as I say,
  "Oh, *stop!*"

I'll miss you, Jan.

In loving memory of my friend Janice "Jan" Crouch.
March 11, 1957 - July 9, 2012

Clarity

In a moment of inattention
the small china horse falls to the floor
   in
       slow
            motion

    s h a t t e r i n g

and the tears fall

Tears
     for time lost,

     for dreams lost,

     for hope abandoned;

dotting the table as
memories avalanche the heart.

Slowly
   with glue in hand,
   mending begins

   piece by piece.

The horse is placed back into the cabinet
standing once again
the cracks visible
and she wonders

    can anyone see mine?

Broken Glass

You spend money
like it's pennies from heaven
and not born of my sweat
as I sacrifice my soul.

Not seeing
the pieces of myself
I leave behind
to give you the world.

Oblivious,
to my heart crying out
in the darkness.

Smiling, you lift your hands
filled with blood covered pennies
scattering them to the wind

while down on my knees
among the broken glass
all I can do
     . . . is watch.

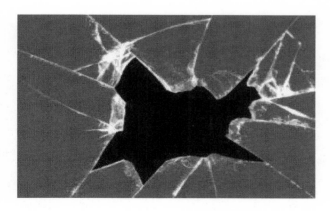

Time

Time drips off the roof in
the darkness outside my window

splashing on the sidewalk, like
children jumping in water puddles.

I catch the drops but no matter how
tightly I hold them, the minutes slip away

pale moonlight creating a street filled
with twinkling rainstars.

A precious few I press between the tattered pages
of my life; those I cannot bear to ever be without

    minutes spent with you.

I hold the book tightly pressing it to
my cheek; the cover wet with rain

    or is it my tears?

and still

time drips off the roof in
the darkness outside my window.

The Promise

Lost within the valley of darklings
fluttering on broken wings, deep

heartache stealing labored breath
eyes glazing from incomprehension.

Hopeful wings beat a staccato rhythm upon
the ground as flames of resignation
try to claim a sacrificed soul.

A haunting melody slowly fills
the downtrodden heart.

Soon, from deep within Phoenix rises; new
strength coursing through defeated veins
healing what was once thought vanquished.

No longer a fading memory,
you hear my voice
whispering:
   I promise
      to sing to you.

Everything's OK

In the bathroom mirror
the old woman is in the way
and I fret because she won't move
but then
    I hear you say
        everything's ok.

My clothes fit a little tighter
they must shrink in the wash
but you say
  I love your little belly
        everything's ok.

I try to love you like a porn star
but that's just not my way
you just smile and hold me tighter
whispering
        everything's ok.

Time goes faster as I get older
and the thick air slows me down
my heart sinks like a stone.

    Still

in your eyes I remain
all you've ever dreamed of
and with your words
my heart takes flight

then I hear you say
    honey
        everything's ok.

The Awakening

Asleep

immersed in halcyon dreams
tight hugs beneath a sapphire sky

velvet words splashed with passion
float in sparkling laughter.

Giving of all you are
    of all you have
        because

that's what love does while
singing heartsongs amid
    smiles
        upon smiles
            upon smiles.

Then the dawning

tossing and turning as rose colored sky fades
moaning
        Why?
arms flailing in the tangled sheets of confusion
        Why?
promises unfulfilled.
        Why?
Because love is not equal
    or fair.

Here endeth the lesson.

I don't want to learn,
    for now I feel the pain
        upon awakening.

Shades of Gray

Black and white, and shades of gray
that's how I will remember you.

Dove gray the car, leather seats off-white
black the clouds that boiled from the storm.

White was the song my heart sang to you
black was your despair
gray were the words we dared to speak.

Pale white the light that spilled through the door
black our shadows intertwining
gray the perfect blending as your hungry lips met mine.

Black was the bed where I laid my head
on soft white pillow mountains
gray were the sheets, cool against my skin.

Pink was the blush upon my cheeks
as with mouth open wide
I drowned in your pools of blue

even as my heart was gray
with knowing.

I saw white glowing within your eyes
while ghosts of black swirled around us

and as our lips parted,
and I walked out your door
I knew

my heart will forever beat
gray.

Transition

One sheet
of handmade vellum;
a token waiting for his words
to be placed upon the page.

Harshly crumpled;
tossed into the street.

Remaining

until retrieved by a discerning eye;

gently smoothed out;
loving lines carefully
            inscribed upon the page.

A special dress
hangs in the closet,
            shrouded in plastic.
There was never an occasion.

Uncovered

the fabric silken beneath her fingers;
a delicate touch explores the beadwork.

It comes alive
only when her heartbeat
            is within the folds.

His gentle hand
reaches for the skittish mustang.
Soothing words, spoken low,
                calm a restless spirit.

A toss of the head, a low huffing,
a hoof paws the ground;
understanding and trust
                gain a foothold.

Free, yet bound.

Wild, yet tame.

The fire in the eyes remains.

****

Tony

Pencils and straws and pens,
favorite toys of my furry orange friend.
If left lying about,
there is no doubt,
they'll be hidden by the day's end.

Feather Dreams

Dreams,
soft feathers upon the wind,
I watch them drift away.

Maybe,
someday
in a feather rain
I will hear him say

    Marry me

while down on one knee,
my hand in his,
mist in his eyes as he pleads:

    Marry me

for all the right reasons
and a few wrong;
today and every day
I want you to belong to me,

    Marry me.

Now, in soft white down I stand
as feather dreams around me fall,
I am hypnotized by the cold

of winter's first snowfall.

Universal Truth

Firelight dances in the dark as
I reach for you in our rose petal rain

You slip from my fingers,
and I teeter on the edge
of the chasm that opens at my feet

   every breath your name.

A shooting star in the midnight sky
burns its bright flash onto my heart

   next to yours

and I know
from this moment,
and forever after,

   we are bound.

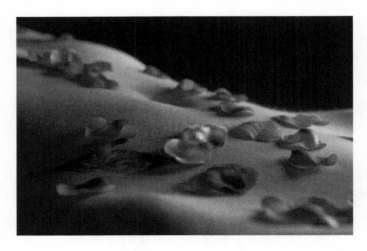

Pinch Me

Pinch me

I *must* be dreaming, for
my last memory of you is goodbye
a pain that seared my heart.

Pinch me

I must be imagining, for
I can still see the dark in your eyes
the dark that swallowed my soul.

Pinch me

I must be delusional, for
I *hear* your hypnotic voice calling my name
speaking words I've longed to hear.

Please,
        pinch me

for I am certain now that I am mad.
I can see that knowing smile, your
eyes smoking as you tell me you love me
as you promise you'll always be here.

I hear it

        I hear the conviction in your voice.

Please . . . don't . . . pinch me.

The Unicorn

Like a shadow stealthily I pass
with but the faintest echo-click of sound
along the paths of dreams and gleaming grass
with silver hooves upon the sleeping ground.

The wind sighs in my wake
and silken moonlight rustles
as I go down all the corridors of night.

I take the way the webs of my desires flow
but though I wander loose I am not free
forever must I listen, ever hear the voice
of her who sought to capture me
an endless mad entreaty in my ear;

for through the night and into fainting morn
love cried, impaled on my golden horn.

Tree of Life

Through all the days of peace and strife
There grows the flowing tree of life.
For no matter what our plight may be
The tree gives life to you and me.
Life and hope and peace and grace
That shows on each believing face.
To take and wipe away our tears
And be with us through all the years.

Celtic tree of life.

Catch and Release

I have to let the minutes go
let them go to where
the minutes go
when minutes are over.

Minutes spent with you
or with loved ones true
not just one or two,
more than a handful,
more than a heartful
then they were over.

Where do the minutes go
when minutes are over?

Are they held suspended in time
aging slowly, like a fine wine?

Or are they like embers in a fire
unseen, yet warm, until they expire?

I have to let the minutes go
let them go to where
the minutes go
when minutes are over.

I fall to my knees
as I catch
and release.

For Lack of a Better Word

All my life
I have walked the city streets
jostled along the way
in a sea of faces
by never-ending sameness.

Somehow
without choosing
I turned a corner
onto a seldom trod path.

Somewhere
beyond the bird's song
or the warmth of the sun
I found a joyful newness
yet so intimately familiar.

I have searched for this path
with the dreaming of a child
the longing of a woman
and finding it now . . .
I have been nowhere else.

Someday
(I promised myself)
my heart would be home.

I twirl with arms open wide
laughing
until I fall into your arms

drifting into peaceful slumber
while you softly sing a lullaby
of three little words.

Standing in Violet

I stand in violet

watching a vermillion sun
   slip beneath indigo water.

Long amber fingers touch my face
   then gently fade away.

I close my eyes,
   willing warmth to return,

longing
to be cloaked in dove gray mist,
the flush of dawn
   pink upon my cheeks;

to lie
upon emerald fields,
alabaster clouds drifting in azure skies;

tangled up
in the golden peace
   of your arms

lost
in the fuschia softness
of your lips upon mine.

I stand in violet

waiting to join you
in the ebony darkness
   of my dreams.

Fade to Black

Standing on the beach
   the sand cool and firm
      beneath my feet.

Waves weave a spell
   their pulsating rhythm
      against my legs…hypnotic
        the wetness…soothing.

In a trance
  watching pink and gold fire
    fade to deep indigo.

Sun slips into night
  her cool chalice
    swallowing
      the blistering heat.

Turning from blackout
    like a siren's song,
   your warmth
     calls to me

for low
  burns our fire
    fiery tongues
      flickering.

To the music
  of the ocean
    we dance

  as slow
    burns my heart.

Echoes

day begins...

reveille, waking upon the cold, hard ground,
    an officer shouts orders

... shut off the alarm clock, throw off the covers,
shuffle to the kitchen

open the door ...step outside
into the silver mist of early morning

....the smoky haze of gunpowder

a car backfires in the distance

....the crack of rifles as the lines of blue
and gray move ever closer

children run and shout

..... impassioned rebel yells

...a cacophony of city traffic noise

...horses whinnying, stomping hooves, the creak
of wagons pulling cannon

a horn blares in angry defiance
... bayonets and swords clash

rain falls; hard wet drops upon the skin

....bullets hit the mark, red stains spread

lights wink on in city windows as the setting sun sinks
    lower

126

...campfires flicker among the tents as men tend to the horses

the endless weaving of threads

another day ends

the journey through time:
                        a circle
                            ...filled with echoes.

My great-great-grandfather Nathan Chew Hobbs
This photo was taken in 1862 when he was a sergeant
in the Army of the Confederacy, serving in Company K,
First Virginia Cavalry, under General J.E.B. Stuart.

Mother's Day

Time marched with leaden feet that day
Seconds ticking by like a dripping faucet
Tick. Tock. Tick. Tock. until he was certain
he would go insane from the waiting.

Time was different back the;
fathers waited alone, while mothers labored
He was no different, foot tapping, waiting
not so patiently for his baby girl.

He was twenty-nine, an only child,
with mischievous eyes, and a ready smile
that only got broader when she arrived.
He held her for the first time, a tiny six pound bundle.

He gave her a Scottish royal name, as was befitting
a true Scot, and she grew in his image; never still
unless she was asleep, so her mother said.
Vaccinated with a phonograph needle, he said of her,
smiling as he answered her ten thousand questions.

Bronzed in the summer with blonde curls,
green eyes that held you steady, she loved with totality,
never holding anything back; her laughter echoing
in the hearts of all who knew her.

The world held wonder and amazement for her.
She walked the railroad tracks with her grandfather;
watched the airplanes with her great-aunt; worked on cars
with her brother's friends when she was older.

But for all her charm, she was different somehow.
She wasn't sure why, or how; she just knew
she was not like the other girls. Intelligent.
strong of character, fearless. Her eyes filled
with a merriment that hinted at an underlying sensuality.

She longed for a date, a first kiss, a hand to hold.
These were given to her for the first time
when she was seventeen- a sympathetic gesture
after the loss of her father.

A Taurus the Bull, she charged into life
with an 'I can do anything I put my mind to' attitude.
She challenged others to 'do it right, and do it right now'.

Unaware that she charmed many, she loved few.
Lived an unassuming life, working hard, caring for her family.
She gave endlessly of her time, her money, her effort,
and always of herself -
for making the dreams of others come true
made her happiest.

Late life she realized that being different
can be a good thing;
a cause for celebration, not resignation.
That as she moved to the front of the line in life,
she found others trusted her guidance,
followed her light, reveled in her joy and the love
and laughter she poured over them like water.

So began the journey for Sunday's child:
fair, and wise, and good and gay;
the precious gift
that turned a beautiful woman of twenty-seven into a mother,
on Mother's Day 1955.

As it was long ago, so it is once again,
and her journey continues.

Author's Note:

Mother's Day began as a poem about my father and quickly evolved into something else and I just went with it. When I finished the work and read it I decided that it was never meant to be seen by anyone besides me. It sounded too personal, too conceited, because it was all about me and it sounded like puffing. But then I realized that it was Mom talking to me from the other side, telling me that I was a remarkable woman. I think she wanted it on paper so that I would always remember how she viewed me.

She has been adamant about making sure I got the message by giving me unmistakable signs that she is still watching over me, and because of that, I decided to share this letter on Mother's Day 2011, which also is my birthday, and the first Mother's Day since her passing.

A few days before Mother's Day while I was back in Baltimore to pack more of her things I found a small notebook of poems she had written in 1944-1945 when she was sixteen years old. My brother and I never knew that she had ever written one word of poetry. I also found this photo of the three of us taken just after I was born. She always reminded me that I was her Mother's Day gift. I take these as signs that this letter was meant to be, and that knowledge brings great comfort.

From my father I inherited the gifts of a positive outlook, a way with words, and most importantly ~humor. I have no doubt whatsoever that any talent I now have is inspiration from my mother, and that this letter is her last gift to me.

The last words she said to me were, "You're so pretty." I believe the beauty she saw was the beauty of the craft which was to come - the poetry within.

Thank you, Mom.
I love you, and I miss you.

Janet

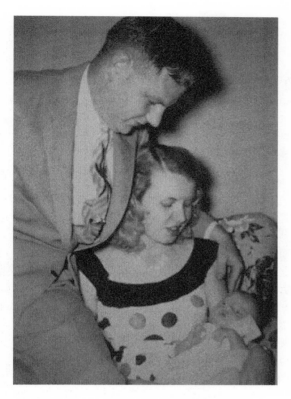

Dad, Mom and me… Sunday's child.

With wick and tallow the fire burns
Yet cool against my skin
I call to those who know the truth
Of the fire that burns within

"Don't ask what the world needs. Ask what makes you come alive, and go do it. Because what the world needs is people who have come alive."　　　~ Howard Thurman

Me? . . . I write poetry.

About the Author

Janet Scott McDaniel, born in Catonsville, Maryland and now a Delaware resident, emerged two years ago from a 25 year hiatus to resume her life as a poet. With an Associates of Arts degree in fine art and a Bachelor of Arts degree in psychology from the University of Maryland, Janet has a rare gift for combining rich imagery with the palpable emotions of human experience and things of this world, both seen and unseen. She weaves ordinary language into poems that are inescapably beautiful but also completely accessible. Her work covers love, loss, discovery, joy and the depths of introspection. She is always looking for an opening to insert a funny one-liner to make people smile.

She currently lives on the East Coast with Steve, the love of her life, her cat menagerie and her angel in black fur, Coal.

Parallel Dreams

Ms. McDaniel's second book of poetry raises the bar set with her first book, *The Light and other Collected Poems*.

In *Parallel Dreams*, Ms. McDaniel draws upon personal experience and inspiration from the other side to delve deeper into the human experience to give us a unique insight to all aspects of life: love, loss, memory, and dimensions seen and unseen.

Ms. McDaniel holds nothing back in her work, and with the accompanying photographs she takes us on a mystical journey that awakens the soul with every turn of the page and leaves us forever touched by her words.

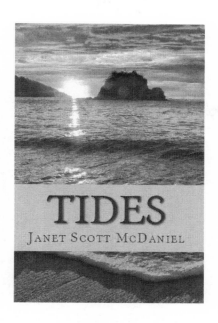

Tides

In *Tides,* Janet Scott McDaniel rides the waves on the journey of life carrying us along with her as she delves into the intensely painful and the deeply loving experiences from which none of us are exempt. The depth of the emotions and the beauty of the images are conveyed through her simple yet powerfully eloquent words.

In addition to her poetry, Ms. McDaniel dips her toes into prose and shares through short stories a few life lessons near and dear to her heart, and a fanciful telling of a real-life experience with a ghost.

Tides will wash over you or lap gently against your feet, but either way it will leave you forever changed.

89560098R00083

Made in the USA
Columbia, SC
23 February 2018